A Dive to Challenger Deep

Written & Illustrated by

Amatullah F. Ahmed

ISBN: 978 9921 0 2482 1

DEDICATION

In the name of Allah the most beneficent the most merciful.
No dedication is enough for our parents. But my mother has been my Mom my friend and best of all my teacher.
Mom, this is for you.

CONTENTS

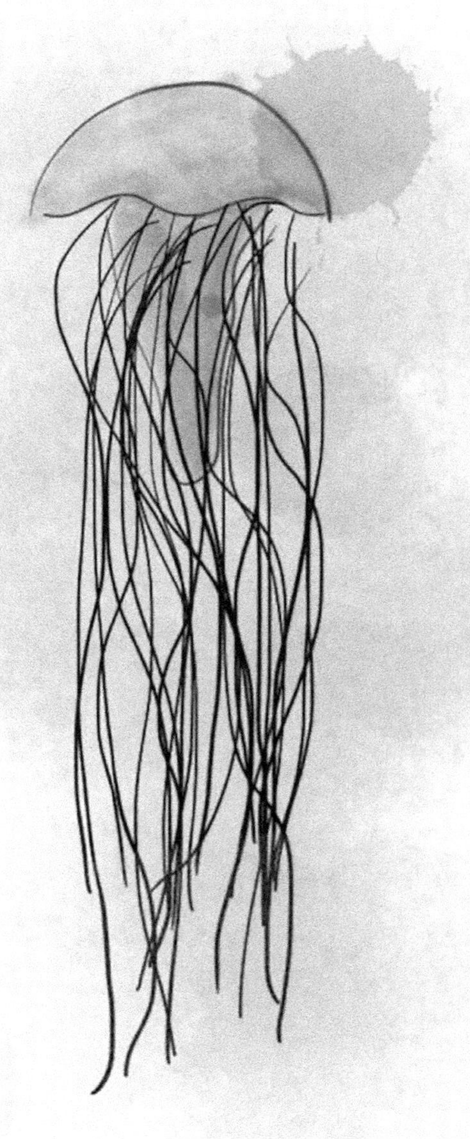

ACKNOWLEDGMENTS

All praise and thanks belongs to Allah, creator of the heaven and the earth and everything in between. We praise and we glorify Him like He ought to be praised and glorified.

I would like to   thank my Grandparents Nana and Nani, who make me feel loved and important. I also would like to thank my uncle Fazal with whom I have long conversations on variety of topics and who always appreciates my writing. Also Nadim mamu-he always makes me feel very clever and special. It goes without saying a big thanks to my little Sister whom I love so much and is so much fun to play with.
And last but not least, my Mom and Dad – the rocks of my life.

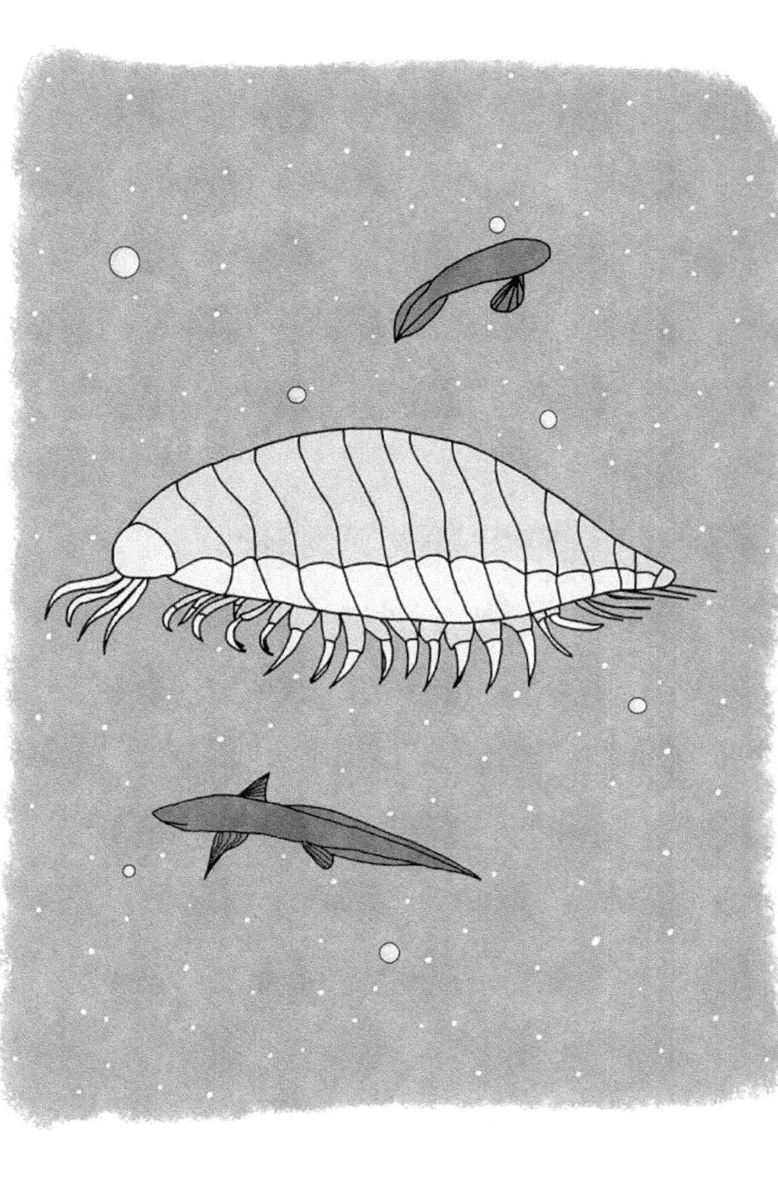

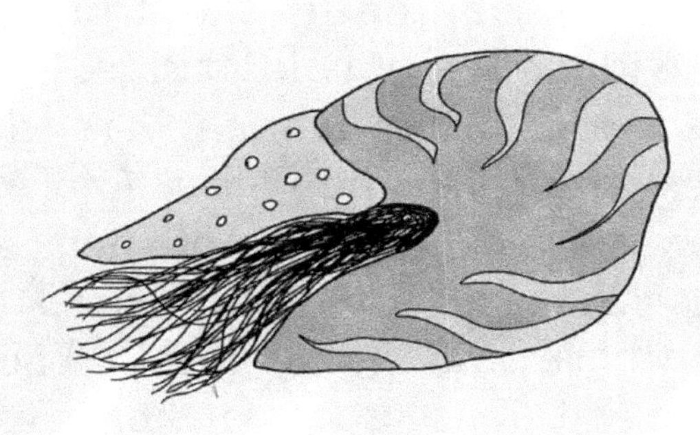

1 - A DEEP DIVE

The three divers, Joe, William and Madison, watched the ship crew lower their brand-new submarine into the water. As the submarine bobbed around in the Pacific Ocean, they all climbed inside, one by one.

Madison flicked some switches and pressed a button. With a *whoosh!*, the engine came to life, and the lights blinked on.

All of this had started with Richard Hemway, a famous Norwegian billionaire, whose ship sank on its way from Japan, filled with chests of gold. It sank into the deepest part of the Mariana Trench, the deepest trench in the world. And Mister Hemway chose the three of them and a submarine called the *Aquamarina* to go down there and get his gold back, in return, a promise to give them twenty-five percent of the gold, if they get it back.

They started to inspect the equipment. "Air tanks?" Madison asked.

"Check." Joe said, while William made a tick in a clip board.

"Deep diving suits?"

Joe adjusted one of the suits. "Check."

William made another tick.

Many ticks later, they where ready.

"Get ready folks!" he said, grinning as he pushed a bright-red lever. "The *Marianas Trench*, here we come!"

The ropes that were holding the submarine to the ship let go, and the propellers started spinning with a soft buzz.

They were off! Journeying to the deepest, darkest and most challenging trench on the face of the earth.

But, it was in the late 1960s, and a submarine expedition to the deepest trench in the world was a difficult and a dangerous task at the time. They had to face many things: intense pressure and possibilities of underwater tremors. And even though most say it is unlikely, some people say that there maybe unknown creatures having their own lives, down in the Mariana Trench.

Their tough submarine, the *Aquamarina*, was small and yellow, with five-inch-thick walls. There were two strong plexiglass windows: one in front of the cockpit and another near the propeller. On both sides of the submarine, there were the ballast tanks. When they filled with water, the submarine could descend; when they emptied, the submarine could rise to the surface. And just beside the cockpit window, *Aquamarina* was written in black, bold letters.

As they made their daring dive into the sea, the water around them became darker and darker. Parrotfish lingered around bits of coral, and they watched a camouflaged octopus attack an unsuspecting crab. Anemones swayed, tiny fishes dancing between their venomous tentacles. Soon, it became so dark, that without the submarine's headlights, they would have been practically blind.

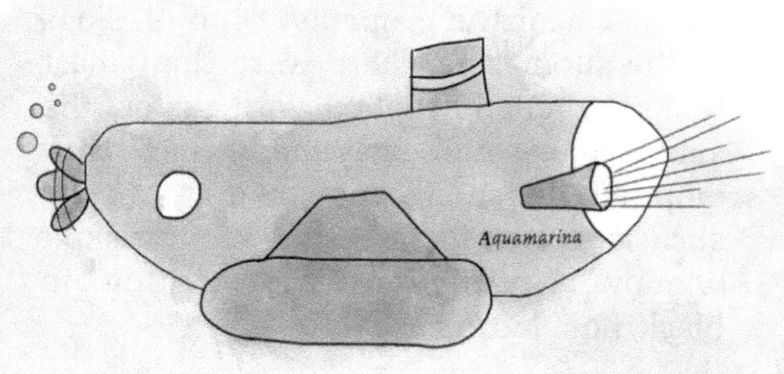

Finally, Madison pushed a lever, pressed a button, and the *Aquamarina's* propellers stopped whirring, staying idle in the midst of a dark, deep world, filled with mystery and water.

"We're here folks!" he declared.

"*Right* above the trench." Joe finished excitedly at the sight he had seen below — a great abyss in the earth that might as well be a black hole in the ocean.

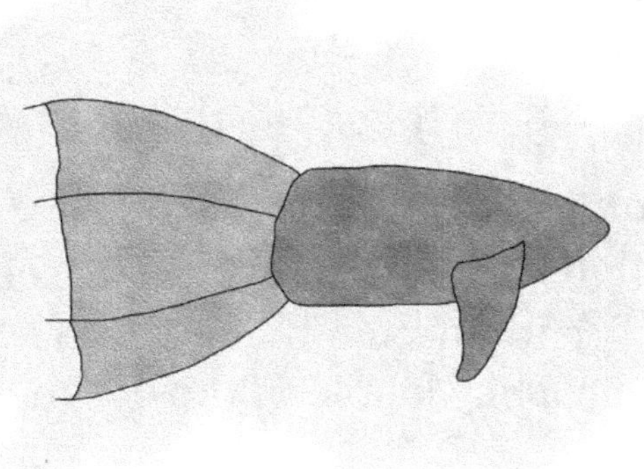

2 - THE PROBLEM

The radio came on, "Coming in!" said the operator. "Can you hear me?"

"Loud and clear!" said Madison. "Yes?"

"According to our estimations, the ship has landed at the bottom of the trench. The plan is that you go down there until you're right above the ship. Put on your special diving suits and collect the chests one by one. Remember: there are ten chests in total. Now, good luck, and, over and out."

Madison pressed a big red button.

"Making descent." said the robotic voice of a machine, and they slowly dived into the dark abyss.

While William was checking a bunch of gauges, Joe was observing the dark world out of the window, watching glowing jellyfishes swim away from them.

Then out of nowhere, a strange-looking squid swam by. When it saw them, it quickly fled, leaving behind a trail of dark ink.

"Wow, that squid must have been scared pretty bad." muttered Joe, frowning slightly.

Except for the squid, he could barely see any sign of life, which wasn't at all a surprise. How could anything live in a place with so much water pressure as here?

But when he looked down, he saw something that made him gasp. In the light of the submarine headlights, a dark creature was below them, so huge that it made their submarine look puny. Joe's mouth fell open, and then he shuddered.

He imagined in his head that the creature had keen eyes and sharp teeth, ready to eat them. He kept on looking down, waiting, horrified for the moment when the creature would rise up and bite deep into the submarine.

But that did not happen.

Instead, the creature wailed a deep song — so deep he could barely hear it — and dived into the depths, where he could see it no more. Joe was starstruck.

"Did you see *that*?" he gasped.

"What?" William asked, looking up from the water pressure gauge.

For a few moments he could not speak. He shook his head to recover himself. "That creature, it was huge! It could've eaten the sub!"

"What are you talking about? Joe, we can barely see any *fish* down here, let alone some giant 'creature'."

"Madison!" Joe nearly wailed. "I'm sure you saw it, right!? It was more than huge, and—"

"Actually, no." Madison said, calm as a sea cucumber. "I didn't see anything, except a few jellyfishes. It must have been your imagination."

Joe made an exasperated sound. "Well...
—"

But before he could finish, the submarine shook violently. The water swirled around them, making their submarine spin around in crazy circles, before crashing tail-first into the rocks with a loud and agonizing *CRUNCH*.

The collision made Joe and William crash into each other and collapse to the ground.

"Hey! What's happening?" yelled William.

"A tremor!" Madison replied as he was struggling to steer their submarine. He strained and pulled and jerked the wheel, but the submarine did not respond. "Oh, move already!" he grumbled.

As if answering, the machine said, "Warning: engine failed."

Madison groaned. For a moment, he looked helplessly at the flickering lights of the buttons. He turned on the radio. "Hey, Operator! Come in!"

The radio turned on, but the radio was crackling and hissing, and the operator's voice was cutting off randomly. "Coming...

in! Listen... weak... contact... detected... tremor! Head... for.. open... water!"

"We can't!" Madison nearly yelled over the hissing microphone. "The engine's broken!"

"Repeat... Losing contact! In three... two... one..."

The radio went silent.

Madison banged the radio. "Hello? Hello! Can anyone hear me?" But it was no use. Their contact had been cut off.

"Help's coming, right?" Joe asked in a shuddering voice. He was hugging William out of fear.

"No." Madison said. "We lost contact."

Suddenly, a rock whammed into the *Aquamarina's* window, and, with a yelp, Madison crashed into William and Joe. The beat-up submarine did five full somersaults before coming to a stop. The three divers sat still, while the lights flickered and turned off, and a million different alarms kept blaring. All the while, the *Aquamarina* was sinking faster with every second.

"We're doomed." William said in the gloomy darkness.

"That is, if we don't *do* something." said Joe.

"I know what to do," said Madison. "put on your diving suits, and *abandon the ship*."

So that was what they did. They hurriedly put on their suits and William tried to open the door of their submarine.

"It's no use!" he said. "It... won't... budge!"

"Do you feel something?" asked Joe.

"WHAT?" William and Madison shouted together.

"Is it just me, or did this thing stop going down? It feels like we're going *up*."

They all stayed silent for a few moments, and he was right. It felt like as if something *was* lifting them up.

"Up!" a loud voice boomed. "Up, up! Ya all see that lil 'cave? Yeah, there!"

With a loud *thump!* the submarine landed on smooth, hard rock. They glanced at the cracked window, and there, glaring at them was the shadow of a small, ugly-looking fish.

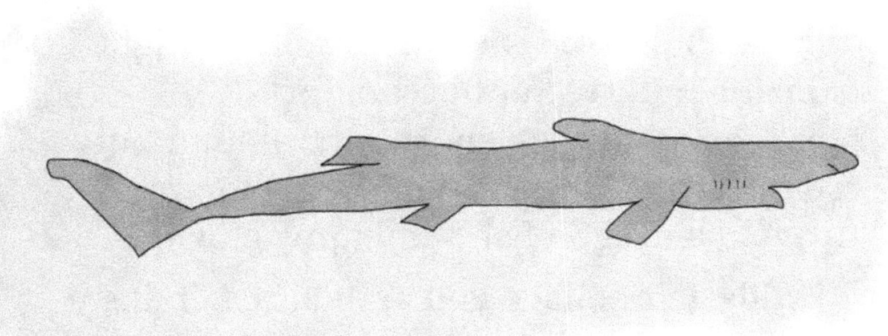

3 - THE CREATURES

Joe, William and Madison all sat in the cave, with rocks on either side of them. Animals glowed and glittered in the cave, lighting it up. Not too far away from them, their submarine stood while creamy-white amphipods crawled all over it in search of food.

And there, in front of them, an ugly fish scowled at them. He was about the size of a teacup, dark red and round, with small fins and terribly big teeth. His teeth were so long, his mouth couldn't even close. Dangling in front of his face was a long, rod-like thing where, at the end, it glowed.

The fish looked like he came straight from an underwater horror story.

Joe gaped at the enormous amount of creatures in the cave, while Madison tried to avoid a dragon fish's unhappy glower.

"I still can't believe you animals can talk." murmured William.

The fish frowned at him, and mumbled

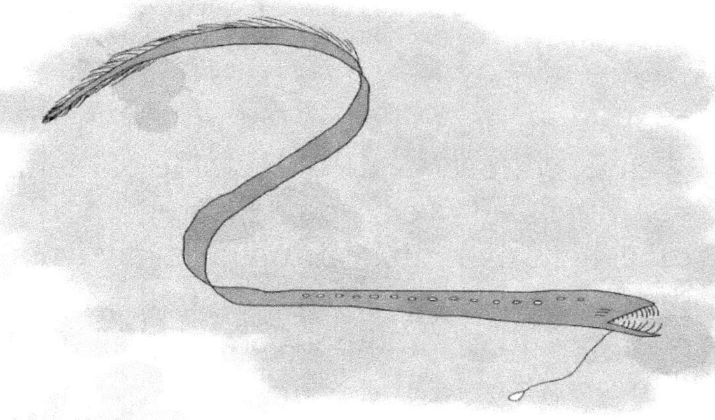

something under his breath. Behind him, they could hear the creatures whispering in hushed voices. The creatures were of all types and sizes, from a tiny lantern shark that was zipping around in what seemed like anxiety, to a giant bigfin squid that managed to squeeze into the cave, its tentacles dangling from above. Some snailfish and a telescope octopus quietly kept their distance.

They didn't look too dangerous, but they didn't seem to be happy either. It stayed quiet in the cave for a long time.

"Well, if you don't mind me asking," Joe said, surprisingly breaking the silence. "but how come so many of you guys live here? I mean, when *we* were coming down here, there was barely anything!"

The fish frowned at him. "A vampire squid saw you and told us about it. We were hiding."

Joe remembered the spooked squid he had seen before. "Wait, you were *hiding*?" he asked, disbelief in his voice.

The fish snapped, squinty-eyed, "Why do *you* care? You're just lucky we saved you. Now, tell me what you want, and get outta here!"

"Why do you want us to get out of here so much?" asked Madison in a polite voice. "Is there something wrong?"

"OF COURSE!" yelled the fish. "You humans just throw all sorts of hunk-a-junk that end up here! Plastic, chemical waste, ugh, even *sewage*! And it's not even quiet down here! Your ships up there are deafening. You're destroying our home!"

"Our home!" all the animals in the cave shouted together.

Madison raised his hands. "OK! Easy, easy. Look, we come in peace, and, we don't *mean* to ruin your home. You see, we have a problem too."

The fish glared at him. "Go on."

"A ship sank with some chests of gold, so we need to get them back. But, our sub, well... the engine's a little banged up, so we need some help. We don't mean any harm. We just need to get the gold back."

"I have one condition before you can do that," said the fish. "you have to promise, promise, *promise* that you will not tell about us and keep our secret." He paused for a moment, and then said in a softer voice, "We want to keep our home safe."

The three divers gave each other knowing looks and turned to the fish. "We promise." they said in unison.

"Do you really?" the fish asked suspiciously.

"We promise with our honor." said Madison. Joe and William nodded.

The fish looked at them for a few moments, and then he and the other creatures huddled in a circle, whispering, while the divers looked at each other quizzically.

Finally, the fish turned to them. He did not look unhappy anymore. He was smiling, even though it looked sort of like a scowl, with all those teeth sticking out of his mouth. "Fine then. Your promise has been accepted. I may as well introduce myself: you can call me Bigmouth, the anglerfish."

"And our names are Joe, William and me, Madison." said Madison.

All the animals cheered and tiny jellyfish and firefly squid started to glow and dance all around them.

"Well, that's over." murmured Joe.

"Just one thing: how will we get the gold *now*?" whispered William.

Madison thought for a few moments. "I know! The sea creatures can help us!"

"How?" asked Joe.

"Simple: teamwork."

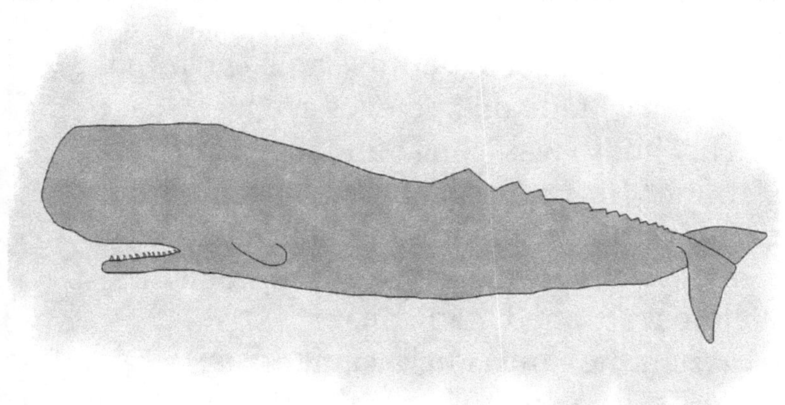

4 - THE MISSION

Bigmouth looked at Madison. "That's the plan, eh?" The anglerfish turned to the other animals. "Ya got it, gang?"

All of the animals nodded.

Bigmouth turned to Madison with a grin. "You'll love this part. Follow me."

He led the animals and the three divers out of the cave and then yelled out, "Mi-ick!"

A loud bellow from below answered and then out from the depths came the largest creature Madison had ever seen.

His body was long, and his head was round. He was bigger than a school bus! The whale blasted loud clicks at them as he rose. The clicks were so loud, they almost stunned Madison.

When he and Mick came face-to-face, Madison suddenly realized that this creature in front of him was a monster of a whale.

"Meet Mick, the sperm whale." introduced Bigmouth "A very good diver." He turned to Mick. "And these are my new friends, William, Joe and Madison. "

Joe looked at Mick carefully. He whispered to himself, "Hey, wait a sec! You're the creature I saw!" He shuddered, then nudged Bigmouth as far away as he could. "You sure he not gonna eat us right now? Look at him! His teeth are as big as my *hand*!"

The huge whale bellowed out a laugh. Joe looked at him, surprised. "You heard me?"

Mick blew a stream of tiny bubbles through his blowhole, and he smiled a friendly smile. "I don't hurt humans." His voice was deep and musical, almost like a cello. "I eat squid, mostly."

"OK," Joe said carefully. "That's good."

"Whoa." said William, astonished by the sheer size of the whale. He didn't seem scared at all. "You must be the biggest creature on Earth."

Mick laughed again, "Then you haven't seen the Blue Whale, the mightiest of them all. Compared to me, I'm only half his size! And you would feel as small as a shrimp in front of him — he equals fifteen humans in length." he showed his back to them. "Have a ride. It's fun."

William, Joe and Madison all went on his back, and with the other animals following behind them, they went down.

Bigmouth went by their side. "So the ship's at the bottom of the trench?"

Madison nodded.

Bigmouth froze. So did Mick and the other animals. "Oh... but there's a problem." he said.

"What?"

"Hydrothermal vents."

Joe raised his hand, "One question: what is a hydra… hydro… something?"

"Hydro-thermal-vents," said William, pronouncing the word. "They're basically undersea volcanoes."

"We feel they might erupt soon. We have to be quick." explained Bigmouth.

"I have two more questions," said Joe.

"First of all, what is that rod thing on the top of your head?"

"Call it a lure. It's for hunting." said Bigmouth.

"And how do you animals *glow*? It's quite amazing."

"Bioluminescence."

"Bio-what?"

"More swimming, less talking."

So they all swam again, deeper, faster. Finally they reached the ship wreck, curious creatures slinking around it, ever hopeful to find something delicious. Not too far away were the tall, black vents, spewing warm, mineral-rich water that mixed with the cold ocean.

"Here." announced Madison.

Bigmouth turned to all the octopuses in the group. "You heard him." he said.

"Search around for chests. There should be ten of 'em."

"Wait a minute," said Joe. "What about the jellyfish and the eels and the other creatures?"

"They'll give light." said Bigmouth. "That's just as important."

"Where we'll keep the chests, again?" asked William.

"Over there." explained Madison, pointing his finger to a cliff not far away.

"Well, what are we waiting for?" said Bigmouth. "Lets get searching!"

So all of the animals swam inside the ship, including Joe, William and Madison.

One by one they found the chests and tied it to Mick's back with ropes.

"The octopuses say there's one more left. Follow me." said Bigmouth to Madison. They both went inside. After searching through almost every room, Madison broke through a creaky door, and there, among all the wreckage, they found the chest, along with a strange creature sitting on it.

It looked like a crab. A big, white crab with fuzzy arms. Madison stared at it, both horrified and amazed.

"Who's there?" asked the crab, suddenly waving his claws.

"Don't worry." said Bigmouth to Madison. "That's Lorris, the yeti crab." He turned to Lorris. "It's just me, Bigmouth. And this is my new human friend, Madison."

"Oh, well, nice to meet ya." Lorris said. He extended out an arm for a claw-shake but accidentally pinched Madison.

"Nice to meet... Ouch!" he yelled

"Oh, sorry," said Lorris. "I can't see, so I'm not so good with claw-shakes."

"Wait, you're blind?" Madison gave him a look.

"Yeah. But what's the use with eyes when there isn't any light?"

"Hey, Lorris," said Bigmouth. "Ya better get outta here. The vents are erupting again."

"Sure. Well, anyways, bye."

He scuttled off to some loose floor boards as Madison shook his head.

The Mariana trench has to be one of the strangest places on Earth! he thought.

He glanced at Bigmouth. Before, Madison would have thought that the angler fish had come out of a monster story. But now, he realized, you cannot judge everything from the outside. Bigmouth was, in fact, a normal fish, and of course he wasn't evil, even if his looks said the opposite.

He lifted the chest, and together, Mick carried all the chests to the cliff. Suddenly, the sea-floor shook with a deep rumble, and red-hot lava creeped towards the ship.

William started counting the chests. "One... two... three... wait... Where's ten? There's only nine!"

"What?" Bigmouth turned to the octopuses in the group, questioning and scolding in a grumpy voice.

Madison looked around. "And where's Joe?" Suddenly, the realisation hit him: Joe was still in the ship.

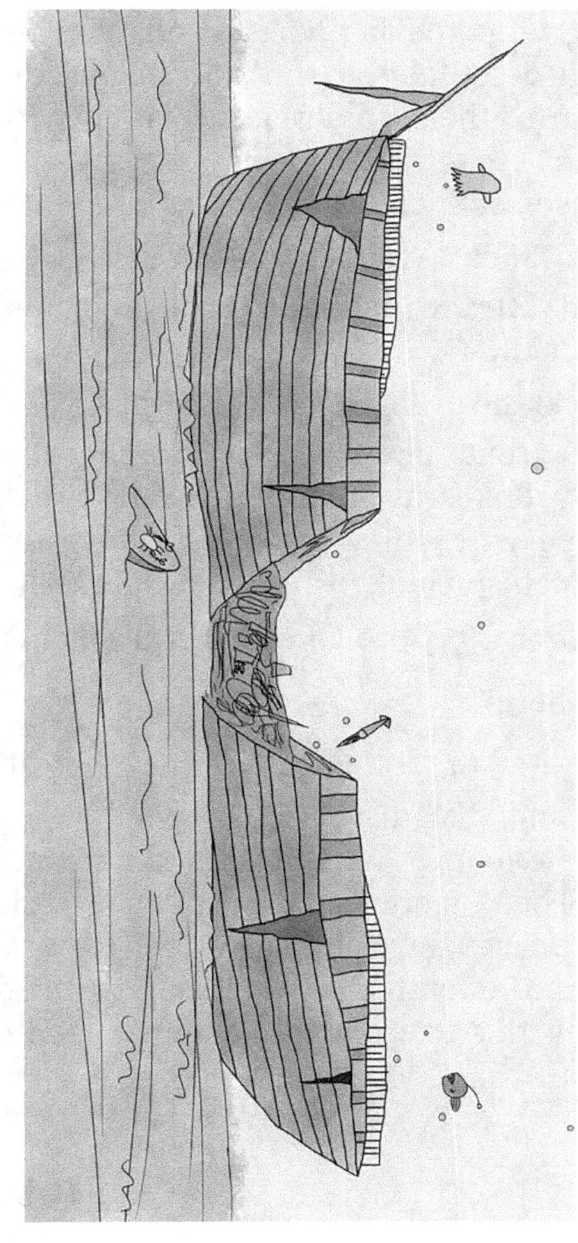

Along with the last chest. All of them looked dreadfully at the ship below, the bottom of the ship already covered with lava.

Madison suddenly had an idea.

"Hey, Mick!" called out Madison. He leaped off the cliff and Mick swooped under him.

"Quick!" he ordered. "To the ship!"

Mick went downwards, pumping his mighty flukes as fast as he could. They stopped when they were just above the ship. Madison looked around desperately.

Suddenly, Joe's voice called from below.

"Over here!"

"There! Go towards the voice!" commanded Madison.

Mick swooped down, streamlined and fast. Then, among the wooden wreck, Madison caught sight of — Joe! He was holding the tenth chest. Madison grabbed him by the arm and lifted him up onto Mick.

"What were you *doing*?" asked Madison.

"If it wasn't for Mick and I, you would've been a goner!"

"I had to save this little guy." said Joe. He showed the chest to Madison and inside was the yeti crab, Lorris.

Once Mick had lifted them to the safety of the cliff, Joe and Madison got off. As soon as they did, Mick swooped upwards to catch a breath from the surface.

"The last chest!" Madison announced.

Joe set Lorris on the ground.

William grinned, "Well, it's mission complete!"

"Yep." agreed Joe. He turned to Bigmouth. "Time we go now. I miss the sun anyways."

"Wait!" said Madison. "Bring our sub too."

****

Joe, William and Madison all stood near the edge of the Mariana Trench. William couldn't help looking down at the dark gloom, thinking he was at the top of some terribly huge cliff, and that he was now in outer space. He looked up and watched the marine snow from above slowly settle on his boots.

"You know," said Joe, absentmindedly. "I must admit, it was actually kind of fun down there."

"Fun?" William said irritably. "*Fun*? We almost *died* down there! And you say it was *fun*?"

Joe frowned.

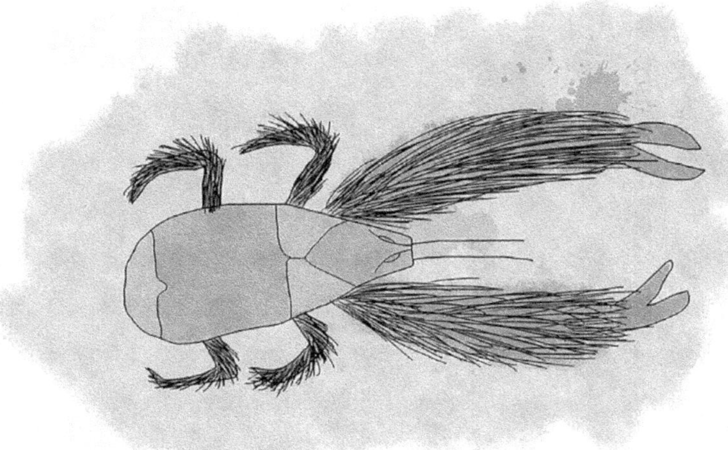

"Look on the bright side." said Madison. "It was fun when the animals came around."

William scowled. "You kidding me?"

"It was fun riding Mick." Joe piped up. "And who's ridden a whale before? We're the first people to ride *a whale*!"

Right then, an idea came into Madison's head. He grinned. "Hey, guys, this is the deepest part of the deepest trench in the world, right?"

"Yes." said Joe.

"And, it was kind of fun down there, right?"

"Challenging's more like it." mumbled William

Madison leaped up. "Exactly! And is this place named?"

"NO!" Joe and William said together, having no idea where this was heading.

"Then why don't we call this place 'Challenger Deep'?"

William and Joe looked at each other with questioning eyes. "Challenger Deep?"

"Challenger Deep!" cried Madison. "It's a great name!"

"It's an awesome name!" said Joe, who was starting to get excited.

"Yes, but—" started William.

Joe was dancing now. "It's the most amazing, awesomest name in the whole wide—"

"JOE!" yelled William. "I'm trying to say something!"

"OK, OK, there's no need to shout. What?"

"The sub operators. What will we say to them? We *did* promise those sea creatures not to tell anything about their secret."

"That's why I told them to bring the sub." said Madison pointing at their floating submarine.

"But wait, isn't the engine broken?" asked Joe.

"The engine broke, but let's hope the rest of it is fine."

The three divers all climbed into the submarine and put all the chests inside. Madison pressed a button and the lights of ship turned on.

"Funny, everything seems alright." murmured Joe.

The radio came on.

"Come in, Madison!" called the operator.

"Coming in." said Madison.

"What in the Mariana Trench *happened*?" the operator nearly exclaimed. It was clear he was trying to keep calm. "There was a detected earthquake, and connection was getting weaker, so we tried to give you a warning, but it was too late."

"Don't worry," Madison informed. "Everyone here is safe and sound. We also managed to get the chests."

"Good, everything's alright." the operator said with a sigh. "We were almost ready to send a rescue team down there! You were gone for hours!"

Hours? All of the three divers gulped at the same time.

"Any damage to the *Aquamarina*?" the operator inquired.

"Erm… the engine is crushed, and the window is cracked. Except for a few dents and scratches, the *Aquamarina* held up nicely."

"All right. We'll send a team down there to help you. I'll keep close contact. For now, over and out."

They all sighed, and silence filled the submarine for a while.

"Now, tell me: will we really name this place Challenger Deep?" asked William.

"No kidding!" said Joe. "It's the best name for this place!"

"No doubt about that." Madison said thoughtfully.

ABOUT THE MARIANA TRENCH

<u>Discovery:</u>

The Mariana Trench (or the Marianas Trench) is the world's deepest trench. Located south of Japan, in the Pacific ocean, it was first discovered by a vessel named HMS Challenger in 1875. Later, in 1951, the trench's deepest part was discovered. It was named Challenger Deep, after HMS Challenger.

In 1960, Jacques Piccard and Navy lieutenant Don Walsh had been the first people to go into the Mariana Trench with the help of their submersible, the *Trieste*.

<u>Environment:</u>

In the trench, it is dark and cold — as cold as one degree Celsius — due to the lack of sunlight.

Challenger Deep has the depth of 11,034 meters (or 35,876 feet) — that would be like thirteen Burj Khalifas stacked on top of one another from the bottom to the top of the trench!

The pressure in the Mariana Trench is around 16,000 pounds per square inch — a pressure strong enough to crush bone.

Sadly, even with the incredible depth and pressure, people have still been able to find pollution deep inside the trench.

<u>Marine life:</u>

For a long time, it was believed that nothing lived in the Mariana Trench. But when people dived with deep-sea submarines and remotely operated vehicles (ROVs) explored the trench, their findings were both amazing and unexpected. The Mariana Trench is in fact home to more than 200 species, including the sea cucumber, the flatfish, the vampire squid, and a single-celled organism, the xenophyophore.

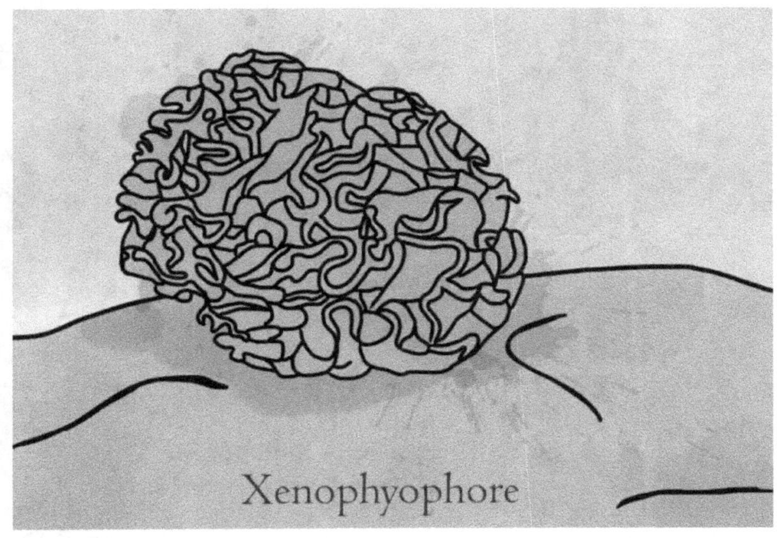

Most of the animals in the trench have one thing in common: they are bioluminescent. This means they have the ability to glow in the dark with the help of luciferin, which is naturally present in their bodies. Otherwise, they might also be absorbing bacteria containing luciferin. When oxygen reacts with this chemical, it produces light.

The lantern shark, angler fish and a few species of jellyfish are examples of bioluminescent animals.

A photograph of the bathyscaphe *Triste*

(Courtesy US Navy Electronics Laboratory, San Diego, California)

The Ocean Zones

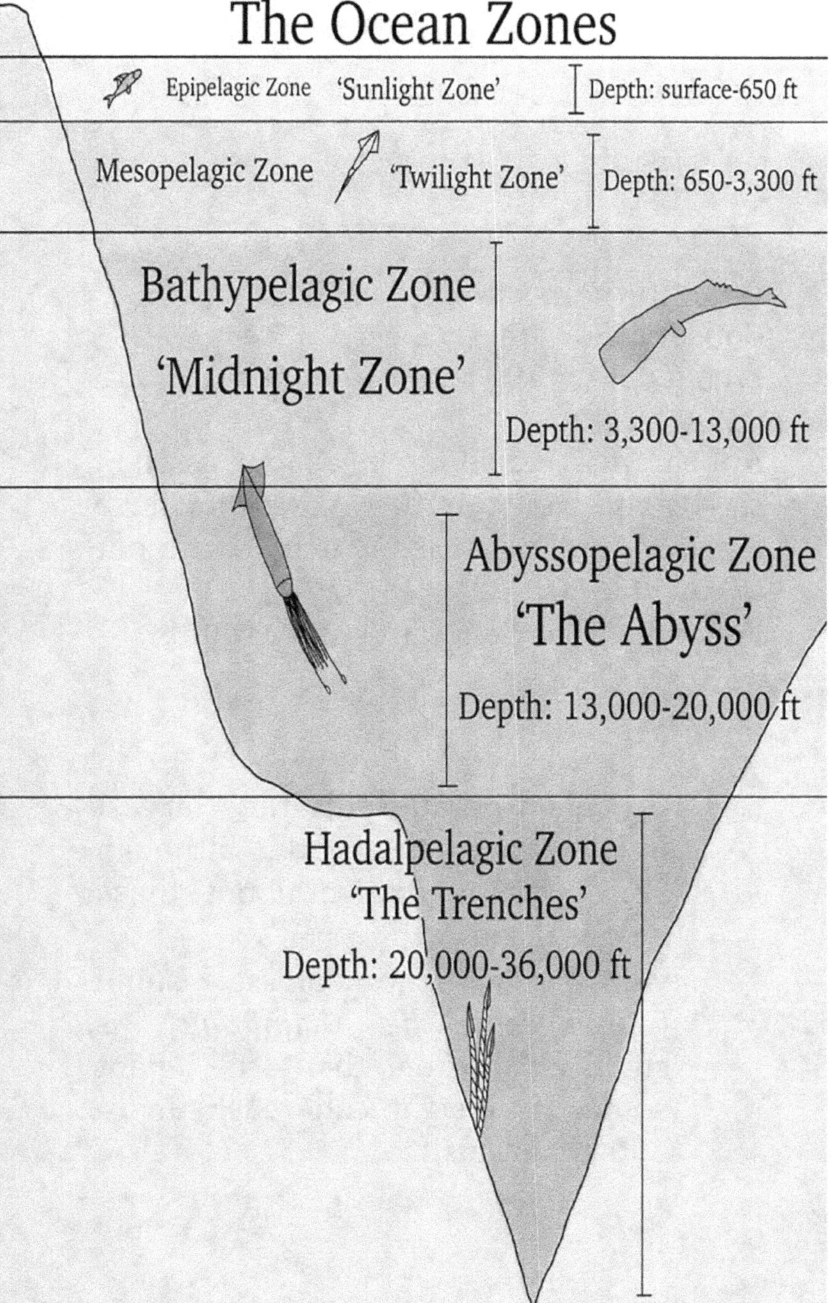

CREATURES OF THE DEEP SEA

Giant squid

Scientific name: *Architeuthis dux*
Conservation status: Least Concern
Living depth: 300 to 1,000 meters (980 to 3,280 feet)
Appearance: Males can be as long as 10 m (33 ft) and weigh up to 150 kg; they have 8 arms and 2 tentacles which stretch out to catch food
Food: deep sea fishes and other squids

Fun facts:

- The giant squid is the largest invertebrate on Earth, although very little is known about these deep-sea giants.
- Even though the colossal squid (*Mesonychoteuthis hamiltoni*) is slightly shorter than the giant squid, its weight can reach up to 200 kilograms!

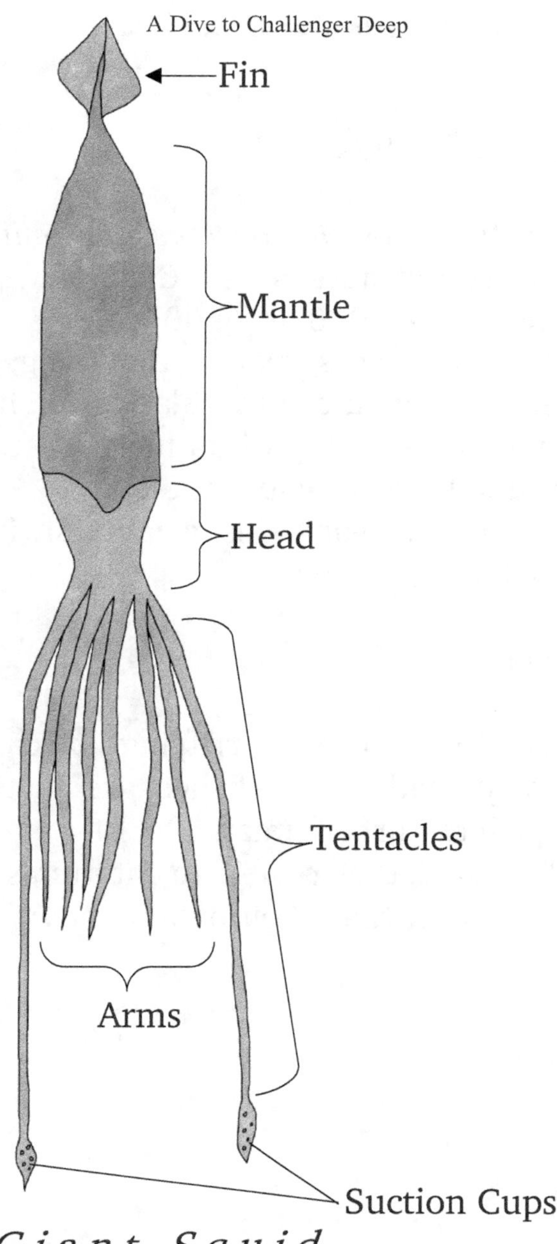
Fin
Mantle
Head
Tentacles
Arms
Suction Cups
Giant Squid

<u>Humpback anglerfish</u>

Scientific name: *Melanocetus johnsonii*
Conservation status: Least Concern
Living depth: 2000 m (6600 feet)
Appearance: Less than a foot long; has dark red, brown or even black skin; has a glowing lure on top of its head to attract prey and long, translucent teeth.
Food: Crustaceans (especially shrimp), small fish.

Fun facts:

- Even with their terrifying looks and scary teeth, anglerfishes are just too small to hurt a human.
- That said, they're able to eat things that are bigger than their own bodies.

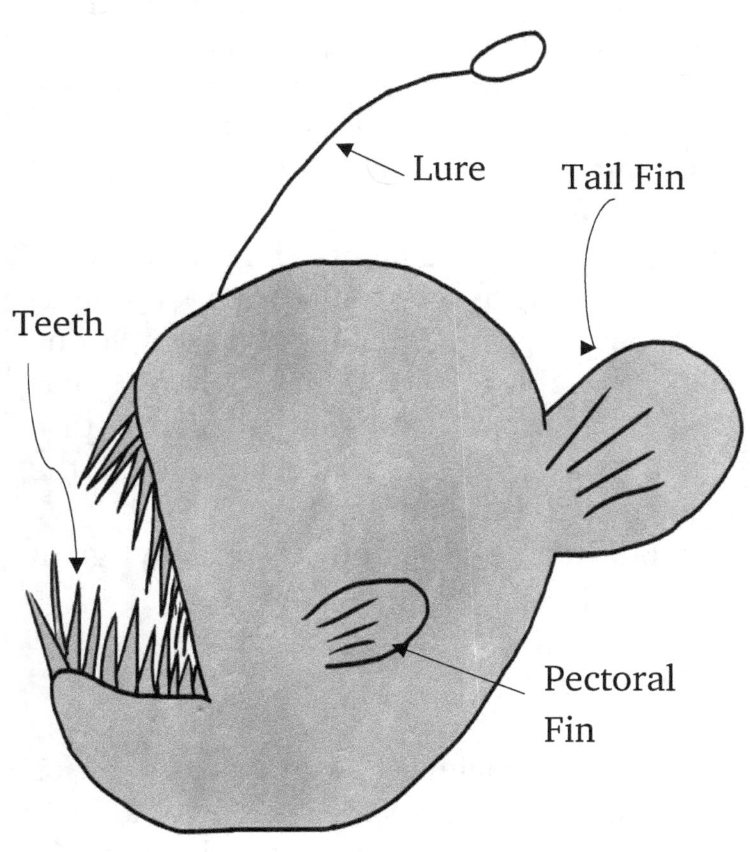

Humpback Anglerfish

Sperm whale

Scientific name: *Physeter macrocephalus*
Conservation Status: Vulnerable
Threats: Fishing gear entanglement, noise pollution, oil spills, vessel strikes
Diving depth: 600 to 1,000 meters (2,000 to 3,280 feet)
Appearance: Usually is dark grey, with males being as long as 18 meters (60 feet) and as heavy as 39,500 kg, making it one of the biggest toothed whales; has distinct, broad head that is filled with a substance called spermaceti, which the whale was once hunted for
Food: fish and squid (especially giant squids)

Fun facts:

- Sperm whale vocalizations can be as loud as 230 decibels — just a little quieter than a rocket taking off — making it the loudest animal on earth!
- A sperm whale can hold its breath for up to 90 minutes while searching for its deep sea food.

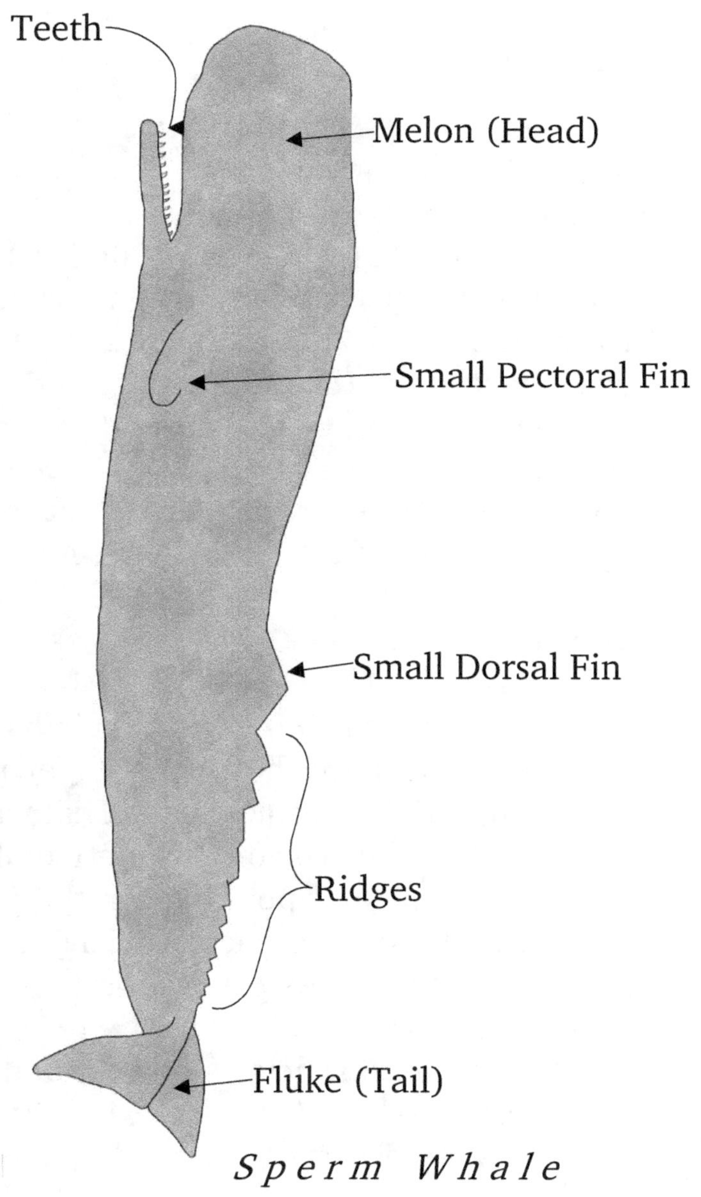

Teeth
Melon (Head)
Small Pectoral Fin
Small Dorsal Fin
Ridges
Fluke (Tail)
Sperm Whale

Yeti crab

Scientific name: *Kiwa hirsuta*
Conservation Status: unknown
Living Depth: 2,200 meters (7,200 feet)
Appearance: It has white or pale yellow colouration, with thin hairs (setae) on its arms; is around 15 centimeters long (5.9 inches) and can weigh around 2 to 5 pounds
Food: bacteria that live around hydrothermal vents

Fun facts:

- Yeti crabs eat by waving their hairy arms over the hot waters spewing from hydrothermal vents. That way, bacteria grows on the yeti crab's arms, making possible for the yeti crab to eat the bacteria. This is an example of chemosynthesis.
- The yeti crab is a recently discovered species — first found in 2005! — so very little is known about these creature.

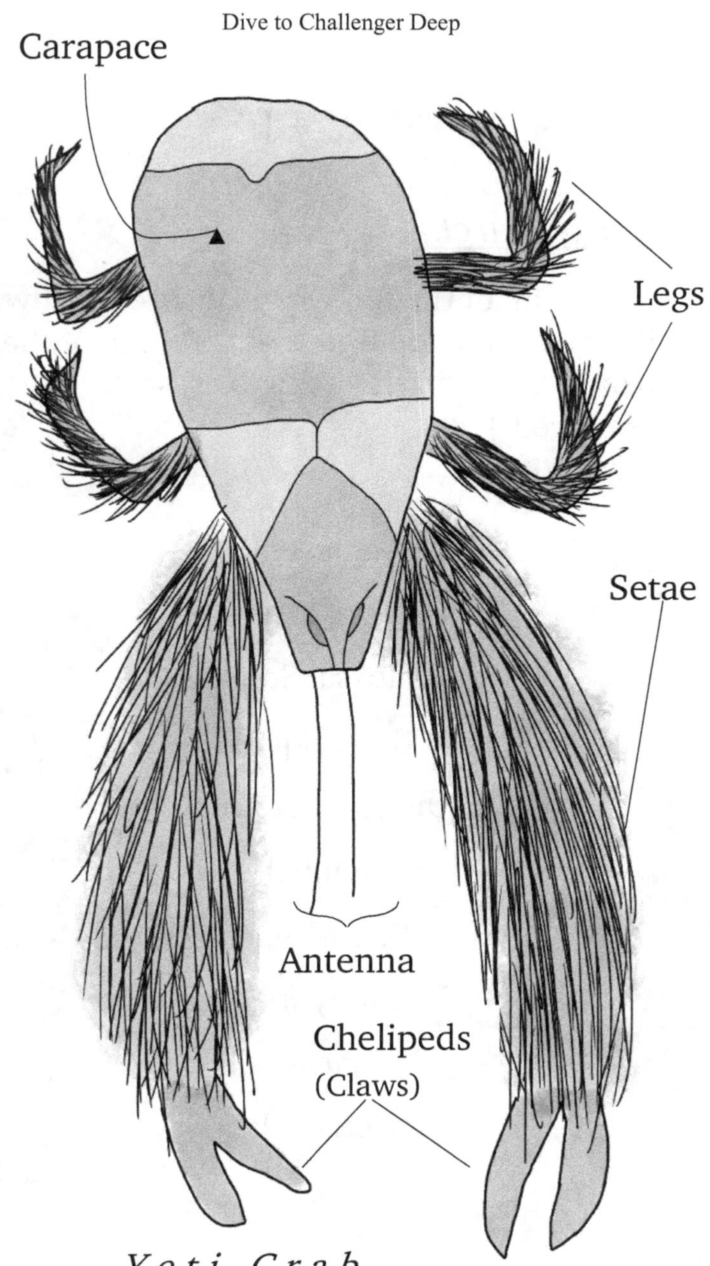
Carapace
Legs
Setae
Antenna
Chelipeds
(Claws)
Yeti Crab

PUZZLES

Word Search!

Find all of the ten words written below. How fast can you find them? (Some of the words are written backwards, so be prepared!)

Anglerfish

Sperm Whale

Colossal Squid

Giant Squid

Dumbo Octopus

Snailfish

Spook Fish

Xenophyophore

Flatfish

Yeti Crab

A g f p w o E V S a j S X D D b z

X e n o p h y o p h o r e u L a V

E r r l p g H h l U p R e m T n S

A b u V q e t Y B v s Z M b k l o

G v W n q t e p h s i F k o o p S

A g H j l t p m G F r Z u O K i n

D n r l i m C H l p b i a c Y e a

W f g C g d f a s h y f l t j E i

h w r l A n t k E o h z X o N i l

q a F h e F l e P e Q H y p w Z F

b B e Q i r y e t I G b n u p L i

l G k s d N f R e E h m T s P x s

f E h n d T G i a n t S q u i d h

E n C o V l D u s Q e T Y S p a K

o f D S p e r m W h a l e b M z j

S a r C B e s n m w k z O z W n p

l m c d d i u q S l a s s o l o C

Crossword Puzzle!

Let's see if you've been paying attention while reading the facts. Using the hints, fill in the crossword puzzle (some of the questions might need some research, so be prepared!).

Across:

1. What is the scientific name for the yeti crab?
2. The __ is approximately 36,000 feet deep.
4. Lantern sharks, anglerfish and some species of jellyfish are __.
5. This whale is one of the deepest diving whales, and also the loudest.
6. This deep-sea beast can grow up to 33 feet!
8. Challenger Deep was named after this vessel.

11. With the help of __ and oxygen, the creatures of the deep-sea are able to produce light.

Down:

3. This fish is common in Challenger Deep. It's named after its flat body, since it stays hidden by hiding in the sand.

7. The yeti crab's food is bacteria, making the yeti crab a __ organism.

9. On the __, Jacques Piccard and Don Walsh dived into the deepest trench in the world.

10. What is another word for these special robotic submersibles had been able to make many discoveries in the deep ocean?

Answers:
1.Kiwa hirsuta 2.Mariana trench 3.Flatfish
4.Bioluminescent 5.Sperm whale 6.Giant squid
7.Chemosynthetic 8.HMS Challenger 9.Trieste 10.ROV
11.Luciferin

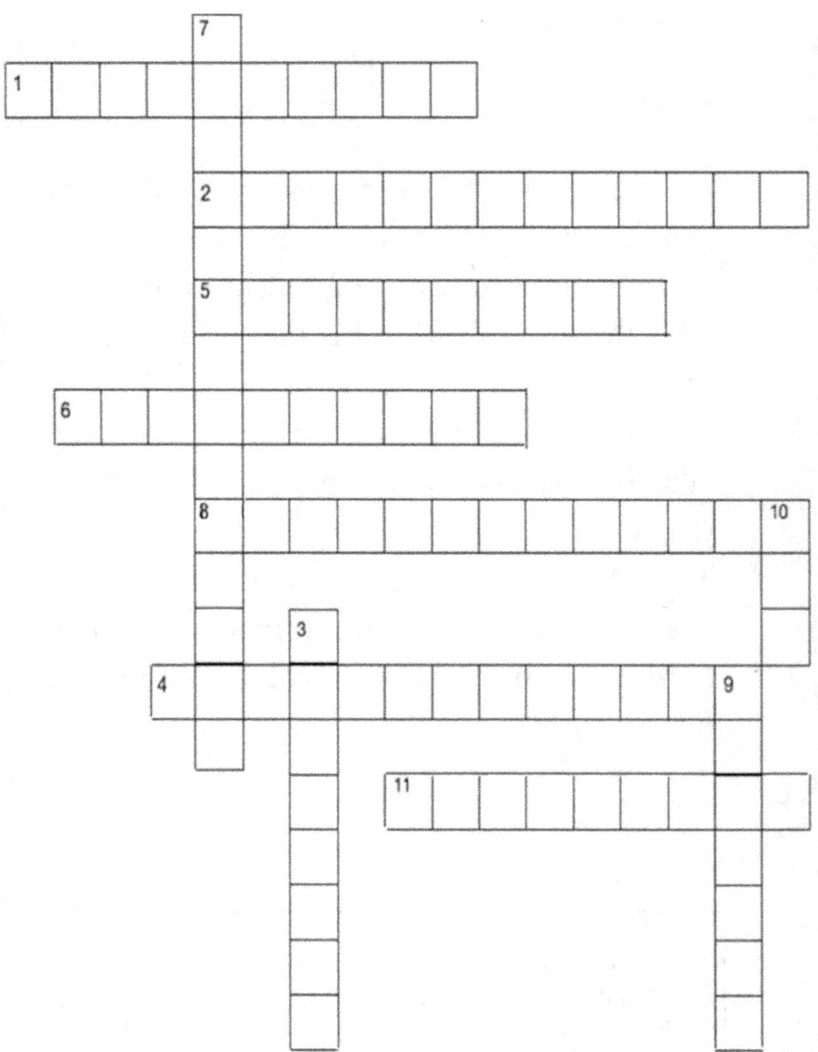

Maze!

It seems like Bigmouth the anglerfish is lost! Can you help him find his way to the cave?

ABOUT THE AUTHOR

Amatullah was born in Pretoria, South Africa. She held a fascination for learning about animal world from early in life.

Creative writing was work, until one evening when she was nine, she had spark of an idea. She turned that idea into a story and since then she kept on writing, writing, writing. Her home environment provided her with ample time to research on her favourite topics.

By publishing this first book at twelve, and In sha Allah many more still to come, she wants to share the knowledge about the creatures of the world.

She drew all the illustrations, typed the story and took the first printout just in time to gift her Dad a copy of this book on his birthday.

When she is not writing stories, she is either illustrating, doing school work, reading, plaster-carving, taking long walks on the beach or eating some dark nutty chocolate.

www.ingramcontent.com/pod-product-compliance
Lightning Source LLC
Chambersburg PA
CBHW061302140726
47998CB00006B/2337